Night Hunger

by

Alan Gibbons

First published in 2004 in Great Britain by
Barrington Stoke Ltd
18 Walker Street, Edinburgh, EH3 7LP

www.barringtonstoke.co.uk

This edition published in 2008

ISBN 978-1-84299-563-1

Printed in Great Britain by Bell & Bain Ltd

A Note from the Author

Funny things, stories. It doesn't really feel as if you make them up. They haunt you like ghosts. That's how it was with this werewolf story. I loved horror movies when I was young, especially the old black and white ones with Lon Chaney as the werewolf. Somehow I didn't just want to write the same old story, though. That's when another memory came along.

When I was 14 or 15 I could eat for England. I don't know what it was, a spurt of growth maybe. Anyway, that gave me the way into my story. My hero is a typical teenage lad. He is hungry and he is noticing girls. It's something everybody goes through, but when you add a sprinkle of werewolf to the mix you've got yourself a horror story. You've got *The Night Hunger*.

For Robert Cormier

Contents

Chapter 1

Hunger

It's hard for me to explain what the night hunger is. It comes during the evening when the sun starts to go down and the dusk deepens from grey to black.

If there are people in the house I do my best to pretend I'm OK. It isn't easy, I can tell you. My whole body demands food, longs for it, *screams* for it. But there's only so much you can stuff down you before your parents start to worry and ask questions.

It's different when I'm on my own. That's when the hunger takes over. I belong to it.

You should see me. I'll eat anything, and I mean *anything*.

Once, about the same time the dreams started, I ate half a cold chicken Mum had left in the fridge, cold, slimy, bumpy skin and all. Yes, I even gulped the bones down. I could hardly believe it myself but before I knew it I was crunching them between my teeth. You'd think they'd be sharp but no, they went down a treat.

Even then I hadn't finished. A big slab of cheese followed. There was no bread, you understand, just this great, big slab of cheese. That's right, I tore the wrapper off with my teeth and wolfed the whole wedge down in huge, hungry bites. I started on the loaf of bread a few minutes later, pulling off chunks and swallowing them whole.

After that I swigged down a whole litre of milk. It was spilling down my chin and onto my chest when my kid sister, Amy, came in and gave me the strangest look.

"What the hell are you doing, John?" she asked.

If Amy hadn't appeared I would probably have started on the cereal too. I can just see myself holding the box over my head and pouring the dry cornflakes straight into my mouth.

And I would have loved it!

None of the stuff I've told you so far worries me all that much. You see these guys on TV pigging out in pie-eating contests. Nobody seems to think they're odd. What am I doing that they don't do?

My parents don't seem to mind that much. They think I'm hungry because I'm growing.

That's the way it is with 16-year-old lads, Dad says, they eat you out of house and home.

Only it's not the food I'm putting away that bothers me. It's the other stuff, the *weird* stuff.

Last Sunday night my parents had gone out and I was babysitting. Amy was up in bed, fast asleep, thank God. That's when I started feeling the hunger. It came like a punch in the gut. I tried to fight it at first. I picked up a book but my eyes couldn't focus on the words. They just swam about like fat, black flies. I watched TV. Same problem.
The pictures on the screen just didn't make sense. They just turned into a haze of light and colour.

Next minute I was pacing up and down the room. It wasn't long before I had to give in to the craving. The night hunger.

And I gave in big time.

I found this huge steak in the fridge.
I think it was there for my parents' wedding
anniversary, enough for the two of them.
Well, you can guess what I did. That's right, I
finished it off in one go.

But that's not what bothered me.
The steak was raw, you see, *raw.* I gulped it
down without so much as waving it at the
frying pan. I tore through the soft, white fat
and the red, elastic meat. I could feel it
sliding down my throat as if my tongue had
gone down the wrong way.

I saw myself in the living room mirror two
minutes later. There was blood all around my
mouth and bits of raw meat hanging between
my teeth. Yes, *gross*! I was like a wild animal
tearing its kill apart.

When Mum and Dad got home I offered to
pay for the steak out of my pocket money, but
they weren't bothered. Imagine if they'd seen

me chewing it raw though! That would have really freaked them out.

I was worried, I can tell you. I mean, who the hell eats raw steak?

I could cope with the hunger but there are the dreams that have come with it too. They started about a month ago, the night of the school disco.

That night Andrea and I weren't getting on too well. Andrea's my girlfriend. We've been going out for nearly a year. Everybody thinks we'll stay together for ever.

Andrea's great, so easy to talk to. *Sweet* is the word my mum uses. Anyway that night she was getting on my nerves. I don't know why. It just happens sometimes, like when you eat too much chocolate. But I said some bad things. I was mean, stupid. Somehow I liked being like that. I saw she had tears in her eyes and I felt good. The point is, Andrea got fed up and cleared off home. I can't blame her. I don't know what gets into me sometimes.

So there I was on my own, wishing I'd kept my fat mouth shut. I was bored and lonely and I wanted somebody warm to hold. That's when Beth came up. She just appeared from nowhere.

She's new here, is Beth. Nobody seems to know much about her. She isn't the kind who gives anything away either. She doesn't talk about her parents or where she's from. She's not a bit like Andrea.

Andrea is blond and pretty. Great figure too. All the other lads are jealous.

Beth's completely different. She doesn't care what she wears. Her hair is dark and untidy. It looks like she cuts it herself with a pair of kitchen scissors. Or maybe she sticks her head under the lawn mower. You couldn't call her pretty. She's not girly at all. She's lean and flat, not curvy like Andrea, she's kind of ... *raw*. What am I saying? No, I do mean raw. It's a funny word to use for a girl, but it's the best I can come up with.

She's loud and athletic and sexy. She can outrun all the lads, and punch their guts out too, I should imagine.

The first day Beth arrived one of the lads tried to chat her up. He came on a bit strong. Just couldn't keep his hands to himself. So what did Beth do? She threw him back against the wall. I swear, you could hear his bones rattle.

And you should have seen the way Beth looked at him. Her face was white and twisted with anger. That's one lad who is going to keep his hands to himself in future.

No way could you call Beth cute, not like my Andrea. She's got one hard face. She's tough, direct, and sexy as hell.

So anyway, I went outside with Beth. I was feeling sore about what had happened between me and Andrea. I was angry and sorry for myself at the same time. I couldn't resist Beth. I don't feel guilty. How did I know Andrea and I weren't through? It's not like it was all my fault. She was the one who'd walked off in a sulk, for crying out loud. Honestly, what's a guy to do? Serves her right.

So Beth and I were kissing. OK, I admit it. I had no trouble forgetting all about sweet little Andrea. Beth and I, we had our hands all over each other. Our lips were pressed hard together when she did it. That mad girl bit me. No, I know what you're thinking, but this hurt like hell. It was a hard bite. In my neck.

With *teeth*.

She broke the skin. She drew blood. Well, that was it. I just shoved her away and told her she was crazy. I wasn't in any mood to listen to her excuses. I stormed off and walked home alone.

That night the hunger began ... and the dreams.

Chapter 2
King of the Dark Woods

The dream I had after the disco goes like this. I'm walking through the woods. It's dusk. The sun has set but the afterglow is staining the trees and the ground a deep red. The wind is whining and crying through the branches like a wild animal and the leaves are whispering as though they've got terrible secrets to give away.

There's some nameless creature making its way towards me and the trees are trying to bow at its feet. "Hail to thee", that's what the leaves are saying. "Hail to thee, King of the Dark Woods." Crazy, isn't it? But no crazier than a guy who eats raw steak.

My senses are sharper now than they have ever been in my life. I can hear every rustle in the undergrowth. I can smell the damp, rotting leaves on the ground. I even think I can smell the blood throbbing through the veins of a rabbit as it vanishes in frantic haste down its burrow. Oh yes, this whole thing just keeps getting weirder.

That's when I see Beth in a clearing. Moonlight shimmers around her. Somehow I'm not surprised that she's there. She's barefoot, her calf muscles flexing, her toes gripping the earth. She's standing there, tense, watching something. Her eyes burn through the dark.

"What are you up to, Beth?" I ask.

She glares at me, as if I'm breaking in on something important. Her eyes shrink to black points. Then she takes off, running for all she's worth. I watch her go, pounding and skipping over the ground. Those legs of hers go like pistons, up and down, up and down. You can see the muscles pulsing as her feet thud into the ground. She springs, weaves, twists, turns. I want to run with her but I'm feeling heavy and tired. All the life seems to have drained from me, as if she sucked it right out of me when she gave me that bite.

So I stay where I am, paralysed, while she runs off. She's chasing something. I see a shadow darting between the tree trunks, trying to get away. I can hear the catch of breath in its lungs. I can feel the terror in its mind. But Beth's too quick. She moves so easily. She's a wild thing which belongs in the woods. But she isn't like a deer or an antelope. No, she isn't the prey, she's the predator. Every atom of her comes down to one thing. She's a killing machine. She's keen and hard like a steel blade.

Then, in my dream, I see Beth strike.
She twists around and brings down her prey
with a heavy thump. It shudders, corkscrews,
twists in panic. Night birds fly up into the
sky. Moonlight splinters around predator and
prey. The struggle throws up a cloud of dry
leaves, twigs and earth. Through the storm
of dust and debris I can see two shadowy
figures. Beth's got her victim in a tight grip,
a kind of embrace. The victim's limbs are
lashing out helplessly, moving this way and
that, but not for long.

Suddenly I want to get away. I try to
move but can't. What kind of dream is this?
It's so clear. There's nothing fuzzy or blurred
about the pictures I've got in my mind.
The whole dream's as real as the bite Beth
gave me at the disco.

I start to make my way towards Beth and
her prey, creeping forward through the
gloom. I've got to see but I don't want to see.
It's like Beth split my mind in two when she

bit that chunk of flesh out of my neck. One part of me is the guy in the top set at school getting ready for his GCSEs. The other part belongs to the dark, dark night. It wants to go hunting with Beth. I come to within two metres of her. She's got her back to me and she's chewing on something.

"What's that?" I ask.

Beth gives a shake of her head and a shrug of her shoulders. She doesn't want to talk. She's busy. It's the hunger.

"Beth?"

That's when she whips round. Her mouth is smeared with blood, just like mine was when I got that steak out of the fridge. But what's she been eating? Steam is coming off it. I try to look and see.

"Go away!" Beth snarls.

Her voice has turned into an animal growl. It drills through the night.

15

"Go away!"

She's not asking. She's telling. You don't argue with someone when they talk to you that way. It's like the moment when a little kid has pushed its parents just that bit too far. If you're that kid either you back off or you're going to be sorry. So that's what I did, I backed off. As I slunk away through the clinging gloom I still didn't know what it was that Beth had caught.

I wasn't really curious though. No, that wasn't why I wanted to see what she'd got. I was trying to get closer because I wanted my share.

I was hungry.

Chapter 3

Beth

I made it up with Andrea on the Saturday, the day after the school disco.

"Sorry," I said.

The big word.

Sorry.

Andrea talked a lot. I listened. Then I talked a bit and she listened. I was so guilty about Beth I nearly started crying. Then Andrea and I kissed. That was the best part.

I love making up. She kissed me on the lips, then gently pushed open my shirt and kissed my neck. Andrea's lips were soft and it felt as if they would heal my neck.

Andrea drew back. "What did you do to your neck?" she asked. She had seen the bite mark.

"It's nothing," I told her.

"Nothing? The skin's all broken and bloody. It looks really sore. Are you sure you don't need stitches?"

I shrugged so Andrea stopped talking about it but I could see she didn't look too happy.

On the Sunday they found Mrs Fletcher's body. Mrs Fletcher taught French. She was one of the best teachers in our school, one of the nicest too. She didn't deserve it.

Loads of the kids were crying that Monday morning. Who could have done such a thing

to Mrs Fletcher? They'd found blood on the driver's seat of her car and more leading away from it, towards the woods.
The bloodied footprints carried on right into the trees. It looked like she'd been attacked in her car and finished off in the woods.

Anyway, you could hardly hear the Headteacher's assembly for the sound of crying that Monday morning. All the girls were at it, all except ... Beth. She just stood there looking straight ahead. There wasn't a flicker of feeling in that hard face of hers.

She must have seen me looking at her, because her head whipped round to look at me. When her eyes met mine my blood ran cold. I saw the same look I'd seen in that weird dream of mine. The eyes were points of darkness.

It was a hunter's look.

The moment the assembly finished I went right over to Beth. I knew Andrea wouldn't like it. She had a feeling that there was some sort of connection between Beth and me. But I just had to say *something*.

"It's a terrible thing to have happened," I said.

"What is?"

"Mrs Fletcher, of course," I answered. "I mean, her being *murdered*."

"I didn't like her," Beth said simply.

She used to talk that way a lot. She didn't sound like a teenager then. She was more like a kid, a wild child.

"Just because she gave you that detention?" I asked.

The bust-up last term between Beth and Mrs Fletcher flashed into my mind. Beth swore in class. She had called Mrs Fletcher something. So Mrs Fletcher gave Beth half an hour's detention after school. Beth didn't go, so she got a whole hour the next day at lunchtime.

"Is that it?" I said. "You're acting this way because of a stupid detention?"

Beth didn't answer.

"I had a dream about you," I told her.

I found myself touching the plaster that covered the bite on my neck. Andrea had persuaded me to get it seen to.

"That must have been exciting," Beth said.

The way she looked at me made me look away.

"No," I replied, "it was scary."

Beth laughed and started to walk away.

"Don't you want to know what happened in my dream?" I asked.

Beth got to the corner of the library then turned around.

"Oh I know," she said. "I know."

The way she said that made me shiver.

"What was all that about?" Andrea asked, catching me up.

"You know what?" I said. "I'm not really sure."

Andrea watched Beth go.

"I can't believe Mrs Fletcher's dead," she said.

Her eyes were red from crying.

"Have you heard the details?" she said.

Her voice dropped to a whisper.

"She'd been torn apart. It's so ... horrible."

I gave her arm a squeeze.

"It happened on Friday night, the night of the disco," she said. "Just think, John, that was the night we fell out. I was walking home alone about that time."

She shuddered.

"It could have been me."

"Try not to think about it," I said.

"Oh, but we've all got to think about it," she said. "Until the madman who murdered Mrs Fletcher is caught, nobody is safe."

I knew she was talking, but I couldn't hear the words. I'd gone into a kind of daydream. In my mind's eye I could see a body. But I didn't see a human being. I saw ... meat.

"John," she said, "are you listening to me?"

I snapped out of my daydream.

"Yes, of course I am."

"Well, you don't look like it."

"No, you're wrong," I told her. "I was listening, all right."

I wasn't, of course. I was miles away.

It was the hunger.

Chapter 4
Losing Control

Later that night, after I've made it up with Andrea, I look out of the window and there's Beth. What does she want? Why did I ever kiss her?

Why?

Then another thought flashes through my mind. What if she tells Andrea? I go hot and cold as I think about that. I've been so stupid. I've got to talk to Beth.

"I'm going out," I call to Mum.

"Where?"

"Just out."

"What if Andrea rings?"

"Tell her I'm out."

I shut the door behind me before Mum can say another word. Beth is standing under a streetlamp.

"What are you doing here, Beth?" I say.

She's leaning against the lamppost. She's got one foot against it and her leg is bent at the knee. She's wearing a skirt. Her legs are long and lean. She knows I'm looking.

"I'm just hanging out," she says.

Her eyes fix me. She's got this way of looking right through you, staring inside you. She's always in control.

"Sure," I say, trying to fight my feelings, "you're hanging out in front of *my* house. Are you crazy? What are you trying to do, split up me and Andrea?"

Beth fakes a yawn.

"Why would I do that? I can get you whenever I want. I don't have to split you two up to do that."

"You're talking rubbish."

"Am I?"

She moves closer. I can smell her. With Andrea, it's her perfume I can smell. With Beth, it's earth. That's right, she smells of the earth in the woods. She pushes right up against me. My mind is full of her.

"Get off, Beth."

But she doesn't get off. Her body is touching mine.

"Am I really talking rubbish?"

She touches my face. Her fingertips run over my eyes, my face, my lips. I follow her fingers with my mouth. Just when I'm breathing in the smell of her skin, she walks away.

"I'm sorry for you, John," she says.

"What do you mean?"

"You love your Andrea, but I can take you off her whenever I want."

I want to argue but I can't find the words.

Chapter 5

The Call of the Moon

It's getting worse. The hunger, I mean.

I've started getting these awful cramps. They start in my legs. Then they rise through my guts and into my chest. It gets so I can feel everything that's going on in my body.

There's the thumping of my heart, the blood sliding through my veins, the grinding hunger in my belly. It takes over until the whole of my insides are screaming for food.

The need, the hunger, it takes over my mind. I'm up in my room. I should be revising for my exams but I can't read, I can't think. It's as if my stomach has swallowed up my brain. That's all I am these days, a walking digestive system. The thinking part of me is fading away bit by bit. The hunger rules me, the hunger and ... the thirst.

This is new. I've only started to feel this way the last few days. All of a sudden I find myself thinking about blood. That's right, blood. Only I think about it the way you'd think about a thick milkshake, a thick, *warm* milkshake.

When the whole hunger thing started it was the red meat I couldn't get out of my head. Not any more. It's the blood oozing out of the meat that I'm thinking about now. I can almost feel it running down my throat, warm and rich and salty. I can't believe what I'm saying. This is blood I'm talking about.

I'm losing it, all right.

I look out of the window and see the moon roll from behind the storm clouds. It is as though the moonbeams are reaching into me and yanking my flesh with sharp hooks.

The moon is nearly full, a blank, white eye looking down. That means there is more of this to come. There's more hunger, more thirst, more *craving*.

Get your act together, John. Who do you think you are, the wolfman?

I don't believe that old fairy tale!

That's when I glimpse movement out of the corner of my eye.

I watch a cat padding along the wall next door on velvet paws.

Who said you could get up there, you lousy moggy? I want to pull off my shoes and go running right along that wall after it.

I'll show you who's King of the Night, you fleabag.

Listen to what you're saying, I tell myself. *Just listen to what you're saying. Now you're picking a fight with a cat! What sort of weirdo does that make you?*

The phone rings. It sounds shriller than usual. It's as if a caged bird is trapped in my head and it's shrieking to get out. *Let me go. Let me go. To the moon. To the moon.*

Just when I think I'm going mad Mum shouts up the stairs.

"John," she calls out, "it's Andrea for you."

I jog downstairs, glad to be out of my room, glad to be away from the window. Here in the hallway, I can't see the moon.

"Hi, Andrea," I say, trying to sound cheerful.

I need her. I need her softness. I need her sweetness. I want everything to be warm and good and normal.

"Do you want to go to a party next Saturday?" Andrea asks.

I feel a tug in my heart. Saturday. That's the night of the full moon.

"John, did you hear me?"

We've already fallen out once. I don't want to lose her by saying no.

"Yes. Yes sure, I'll come."

"Great. Pick me up about eight."

I put down the phone and stare at the handset.

What's the matter with me? How can I think there is anything to worry about? It's just me and Andrea going to a party.

A party is just what I need to put Beth out of my mind. I return to my room. There's nothing to worry about, nothing at all. It's a party, that's all.

It's just us going to a party. Me and Andrea ... and the moon.

Chapter 6
The Party

"Going to the party?"

I spin round. It's Beth, of course. She's crept up on me. How does she do that?

"What's it to you?" I snap.

"Nothing. I might call in at the party, that's all."

"It's at a friend of Andrea's," I say. "You're not invited."

Beth smiles. Her lips curl, hard, hot and red.

"John, I don't have to be invited. I do what I like. I mean, who's going to stop me? You?"

We're in the school yard. I look around to make sure Andrea isn't about.

"Why are you doing this to me, Beth? Tracking me down all the time?"

"Can't you see?" she says.

I shake my head.

"I'm doing it because that's what I need to do."

"You're sick," I mutter.

She laughs and shakes her head.

"John, we both are."

She bites on her lip. I see the dog teeth sink into the flesh. A single drop of blood bubbles up. She touches it with the tip of her finger and licks it.

"But it's a beautiful sickness."

I push past her.

I think I've got rid of her when she grabs my sleeve.

"You can't wish it away, you know. Our sickness, there's no cure for it."

"Leave me alone, Beth," I say. "You're mad. You don't know what you're talking about."

She spins me round and looks into my eyes.

"I might be mad, John, but don't try to tell me I don't know what I'm talking about."

I shrug off her hand.

"It's the full moon on Saturday," she says as I stumble away. "That's when the King of the Dark Woods walks the night."

Chapter 7
A Beautiful Sickness

It's the next Friday afternoon, the day before the party. We've just had French. It makes me and everyone else think about Mrs Fletcher. The papers are still full of the murder. The latest news is that there were bite marks on the body. The police say body parts are missing. The heart has gone. You don't forget something like that easily. We're all finding it really hard to work.

There is only one person who seems happy. That's Beth, of course. She never did like Mrs Fletcher and she isn't doing anything to hide the fact. I can just see her pulling out her planner and crossing off Mrs Fletcher's name. She's cruel like that.

I look at her and wonder how I could have kissed her. I imagine her lips against mine and I swear I can taste blood. Beth sees me looking at her and makes a face at me. Like I said before, she acts like a little kid sometimes. But she's no kid.

"What are you looking at?" she asks.

I turn around to check on Andrea. She is talking to her friends.

"You," I say to Beth. "What's wrong with you? Don't you feel one bit sorry about Mrs Fletcher?"

Beth snorts.

"What a stupid question!"

"So you don't care at all?" I ask.

Beth leans across so I can feel her breath on my neck.

"Care what's happened to Mrs Fletcher?" she says. "You must be kidding!"

"What are you saying?"

"I'm glad she's gone," she hisses. "So glad."

"That's a terrible thing to say!"

I almost shout it.

My raised voice makes Andrea look around.

"It can't be that terrible, lover boy," says Beth, laughing. "After all, you watched it happen."

I give her a hard stare.

"What are you talking about?"

"You," says Beth. "You just stood and watched while I—"

She doesn't get to finish. Andrea comes over.

"What's going on here?" she asks.

"Nothing," says Beth.

Andrea looks at me sadly, then turns back to Beth. "I don't like you, Beth. I never have."

"Well, boo hoo," says Beth. "You're breaking my heart."

Andrea isn't backing down.

"I'm only going to tell you once," she says. "Stay away from my boyfriend."

Beth laughs.

"You can have him," she says.

But from the look in her eyes I know she doesn't mean that. Then I see Andrea reflected in the dark centres of her eyes. The hunger's there, the thirst too. A thought fills my mind, like a dark stain.

Chapter 8

The Prey

At the end of school that day, I make some stupid excuse. I don't walk Andrea home. I follow Beth. I catch up with her when she's halfway across the park.

"What was all that about today?" I ask, grabbing her arm.

"Don't pretend you don't know," she says. "I can read your mind."

The black pinpoints of her eyes blaze through me.

"I *know* you," she whispers.

I feel Beth's fingers stealing across my chest.

"I know your hunger."

Her fingers have reached my throat. She undoes my tie, unfastens the top button of my shirt.

"I know your thirst."

I feel her fingernails tracing lines across my throat to the gash on my neck.

"After all, it was me that gave it to you."

With those words she pulls the plaster off my wound.

"Get off me!" I cry.

My hand flies to my neck.

"What the ...?"

Where my neck was sore and bleeding, the skin feels smooth to the touch. It's as good as new.

"The bite's gone," I gasp.

"That's right," Beth says. "The full moon is coming. We heal quickly then."

"What are you talking about?" I say.

"Our kind. We heal faster than most people. The moonlight makes us whole."

"I'm not like you," I snarl.

I hate the way my voice buzzes in my head.

Beth smiles.

"Aren't you?" she hisses.

She throws me back against a tree. Her lips are close to mine. I want to kiss her. I hate her but I still want to feel her mouth on mine.

"Aren't you?"

I don't kiss her. I shove her away.

"You're sick," I say.

"Maybe."

She walks a few steps.

"But you've got the same sickness. We have the same hunger," she says.

Our eyes meet and I can read her thoughts. In the dark pupils of her eyes I see Andrea's face.

"No," I say.

Beth laughs as she walks away.

"No what?"

"No, Beth. You had Mrs Fletcher. You can't have Andrea."

Chapter 9

The Predator

That same night, after my talk with Beth, I dream again.

It begins with me pacing the living room floor. The curtains are open. The moonlight floods the room. There is a silvery veil over everything. Time seems frozen, waiting for something. Then I know what I'm waiting for.

It's Andrea.

In my dream she's out there in the woods. Didn't she tell me that it could have been her, not Mrs Fletcher, who got murdered last week? I can't shut the picture out any more. Now I know it was Mrs Fletcher who was lying on the ground. I know it was her heart that was hanging, still pumping, from Beth's mouth.

Suddenly I can't breathe. I've got the hunger. In my dream, I need to eat. I've got the thirst. I need to drink. But my kind doesn't have to microwave its food. My kind eats at 36.9°C, body heat.

My throat goes tight.

"Andrea."

I spring to the window and smash through it. Glass showers around me and I'm running into the velvet night.

"Andrea."

The wind is rushing around me. The earth thumps with the pulse of the night. I am not the only one out here. Then I see her.

Beth is standing far off, a black shape in the rolling mist. She's hunting. I know the name of her prey.

"No."

I watch her starting to turn. She's seen her victim, picked her out. Now everything's happening in slow motion. Time shudders to a halt. Everything seems to shrink inside a crystal of silence. Then, like breaking glass, the crystal shatters. Beth is on the move.

"No!"

She is running and I am pounding after her. The trees flash by. It is as if my feet are hardly touching the ground. The air rushes past. I could be flying.

"Don't touch her!"

Beth doesn't listen. I hear the impact. I see fangs tear through skin, tendon, flesh. A shriek rips through the night. Then a shaft of moonlight splits the darkness. I see the victim.

It is Andrea.

Chapter 10
Blood Sacrifice

On Saturday morning I wake up covered in sweat. In my dream I have looked into the eyes of death. I have also made a decision. I'll get to Andrea's early, before the party.

Her house is at the edge of town, by the woods.

"Hi, you," she says, giving me a kiss on the cheek.

Her lips are warm and soft. Not like Beth's.

"Hi."

I'm at Andrea's front door and I can't help glancing round, first at the woods, wondering if Beth is there right now watching us, then at the moon, the ripe, full moon.

"If we want to get to the party on time we'd better get going," says Andrea.

"What's the hurry?" I say.

"I promised I would help put out the food."

She looks back into her house.

"See you, Mum. See you, Dad."

It's like I'm seeing her say goodbye to them for the last time.

We're turning the corner at the top of the road when I hear footsteps behind us. I hear twigs snapping, branches bending back, leaves hissing against fur. Maybe I'm imagining it, but I even think I hear the hunter's heartbeat.

"Did you hear that?" I ask.

"Hear what?"

No, of course Andrea can't hear it.
It takes a dog to hear as keenly as that, or a
wolf. We have barely gone ten metres when I
hear it again. It is one of my own kind.

"Somebody's following us," I say.

"I hope you're not trying to scare me,"
says Andrea. "After all, the killer is still on
the loose."

Yes, the killer's on the loose. But where
are you, Beth? We start hurrying. That's
when I see her, a darting figure flickering
between the trees. She's coming, my dark
sister.

"What is it, John?" Andrea asks. "What's
wrong?"

"Nothing," I say. "I thought I heard
something, that's all."

"John, you're scaring me."

"I don't mean to. I can't help being a bit twitchy, that's all."

Andrea shudders.

"You don't think we're being followed, do you?"

I don't answer. It is at that moment that the moon carves a path between the clouds. I hear a sound, a wild scream that tears the night wide open. Suddenly I want to feed. I imagine the two of us, Beth and I, feeding.

"What's that?" says Andrea. "John, I don't like this."

I'm not listening any more. The night is stealing through me, bringing the hunger. The moonlight seeps inside me, bringing the thirst. I think of Beth and me feeding, feeding on Andrea.

"John, talk to me."

But the next sound is a second howl, louder, more urgent than the last. Andrea. My hunger is for *Andrea*.

"John, what's that?"

I don't answer. Already there is an answering cry. This roar cuts through the darkness, and it is coming from my own throat. I hear Andrea scream. I see her eyes widen with horror as she sees me, *sees what I am*. But there is no time to comfort her. I can't take away her fear.

Beth is coming.

Soon we will be one. We are of the same kind. We will feast together. Then I scream. What am I saying? The hunger nearly got me. I was going to feed off the only girl I've ever loved.

I've got to fight the hunger.

I have to go to meet Beth, while my mind is still my own. For Andrea's sake I must face the other beast that's like me. I must fight my dark sister, destroy her. I crash through the bushes. Behind me, I hear Andrea sobbing. Finally I see the predator, the killer.

"Beth."

I see her eyes, yellow now. They are blank, unfeeling eyes. There is no emotion in them, only hunger. This isn't Beth. This is the beast, the King of the Dark Woods. Beth is part of him, flesh of his flesh, blood of his blood. I see Beth sniffing the air, seeking out Andrea.

"Join me, John," Beth says. "Let's take her together."

The hunger clouds my eyes. I think of Andrea and I smell red, warm meat.

"Let's feed together," Beth says.

"Never!" I roar back. "I won't let the hunger have me."

They are the last words I speak that night. The next thing I know Beth and I are two creatures snarling and tearing at each other, screaming and twisting and ripping. Bare, barbed toes grip the earth. Claws slash. Fangs snag and tear. The moon looks down on the combat. Which of her savage children will walk away from the fight?

I feel the blood beating inside me. Then I feel Beth's dark pulse too. It is blood against blood, life against life. I can hear screaming and I don't even know if it is me or if it is Beth. Hot blood splashes onto me. Mine? Hers? I've stopped caring. Then my hunger is satisfied. My thirst has gone. I see Beth at my feet, her head turned at an angle, her dark, lifeless eyes staring at the moon.

It is over.

"Andrea," I call, "it's over. You're safe."

I run back to the road and there she is.

"Andrea," I say, "there's no need to be afraid. She can't hurt you any more."

Then I hear what Andrea must be hearing. My voice is still a moon-born snarl. She isn't hearing words. All that she can hear is the night demon, the wolf. To Andrea I'm a monster, just as much as Beth was. Andrea just screams and screams and my heart breaks.

I run back into the woods where she can't see me, where she can't be terrified, where she can't hate me. I hear the sound of police cars in the distance. The sirens whoop. Then I see their lights flashing. It's time I went. I run all night, through the woods, into the countryside, far from home. Just before dawn I find myself crouching by a stream, washing off the blood.

Mine.

And Beth's.

I have made my sacrifice to the King of the Dark Woods. I have fed my hunger.

I look into the water and see my reflection. The wolf is almost gone. The black eyes fade to blue. The dark hair shrinks back into my skin. The claws and fangs slide back beneath my skin. But I know the wolf's still there. It's inside me. I've got to get away, where I can't do any harm, where I can't hurt my Andrea.

My old life is over now, I know that much. Somehow I will go on living, far from the ones I love. From now on I will have to find another way to live, to survive, until I find a way to control the hunger, the night hunger inside me.

Barrington Stoke would like to thank all its readers for commenting on the manuscript before publication and in particular:

Michael Appleby
Carol Barnes
Liz Cairns
Vanessa Evans
Hector Fetherstonhaugh
Lewis Fisher
Jessica Fitzjohn
James Hall
John Haydon
Jessica Hazledine
Wayne Johnson
Jamie Jones

Adam Kemp
Ceri Ellyn Morrice
Alice Morris
Sarah Nesbit
Luke Pearson
Alex Richardson
Alastair Rogerson
Amy Steward
Mabel Stewart
Darren Symon
Stuart Vincent
Jonathan White

Become a Consultant!

Would you like to give us feedback on our titles before they are published? Contact us at the address below – we'd love to hear from you!

E-mail: info@barringtonstoke.co.uk
Website: www.barringtonstoke.co.uk

Also by the same author ...

The Cold Heart
of Summer

Debbie knows the stories about Old Man Sexton who haunts the Grange. But the house itself can't be evil, can it?

When her father starts working at the Grange, Debbie's feelings tell a different story. Outside the house it is summer, but inside it is bitter, cold winter. Can Debbie make her father listen before it is too late?

You can order **The Cold Heart of Summer** directly from our website at **www.barringtonstoke.co.uk**